Kitten's Winter

Eugenie Fernandes

Kids Can Press

For Monica

Text and illustrations © 2011 Eugenie Fernandes

Kids Can Press acknowledges the financial support of the Government of Ontario, through the Ontario Media Development Corporation's Ontario Book Initiative; the Ontario Arts Council; the Canada Council for the Arts; and the Government of Canada, through the BPIDP, for our publishing activity.

Published in Canada by
Kids Can Press Ltd.
25 Dockside Drive
Toronto, ON M5A 0B5

Published in the U.S. by
Kids Can Press Ltd.
2250 Military Road
Tonawanda, NY 14150

www.kidscanpress.com

The artwork in this book was rendered in self-hardening clay, acrylic paint and mixed-media collage.
The text is set in Avenir.

Edited by Debbie Rogosin
Designed by Marie Bartholomew

This book is smyth sewn casebound.
Manufactured in Tseung Kwan O, Kowloon Hong Kong, China, in 3/2011 by Paramount Printing Co. Ltd.

CM 11 0 9 8 7 6 5 4 3 2 1

Library and Archives Canada Cataloguing in Publication

Fernandes, Eugenie, 1943–

Kitten's winter / written and illustrated by Eugenie Fernandes.

ISBN 978-1-55453-343-5 (bound)

1. Kittens — Juvenile fiction. 2. Animals — Habitations — Juvenile
fiction. 3. Animals — Wintering — Juvenile fiction. I. Title.

PS8561.E7596K59 2011   jC813'.54   C2011-900081-4

Kids Can Press is a *l@rus*™ Entertainment company

Snow blows,
Kitten hurries.

Pond freezes,
Fox scurries.

Turtle burrows,
Beaver naps.

Raccoon dozes,
Woodpecker taps.

Rabbit hops,
Mouse zips.

Otter catches,
Fish flips.

Squirrel searches,
Bear sleeps.

Chipmunk snoozes,
Snow heaps.

Blizzard howls,
Kitten struggles.

Door opens,

Kitten snuggles.